HALL OF ECHOES

THE EMALEE LIEON STORY

ETHAN MICHAEL KEAGAN

HALL OF ECHOES

Formatting by:
Elaine York, Allusion Graphics, LLC/
Publishing & Book Formatting
www.allusiongraphics.com

INTRODUCTION

Ana stared out of the double paned windows onto the courtyard below. She longed for the fleeting moments when the sun would warm her skin and the crispness of the air would make her feel alive again. Those moments grew fewer and fewer over the past three years. She could still remember the first time she met Dr. Emalee Lieon. Ana had been a patient of Dr. White for a few years, when Emalee was reassigned to her file. Over the years Ana was treated by many doctors. She hoped that Dr. White would be her saving grace, but soon realized he was like the others. She wanted Dr. White's help, but she needed him to leave. Ana prayed that Robert, her brother would go away with him; however he was always ever present.

Ana would never see a moments rest as long as Robert kept a watchful eye.

Ana leaned back as far as her body would allow in the old wooden chair and closed her eyes. Her mind wanted to reject her reality. Life was overwhelming; it would be easier if she could blame it on the medication. But the truth was that the medication only made things worst. As the effects of her latest prescription begun to subside a little, Ana began to feel jumpy. As much as she hated the medication, it did bring comfort on those nights when the others were restless. It was her only escape from the torment and torture they would inflict on her.

Ana's tactics were recently discovered by Dr. Lieon. For months Ana tucked away pills between the mattress and the box spring. She would hide them to protect herself from Robert. Robert grew more and more out of control and the mattress was a safe haven. If he found the pills he would be furious; but that was a risk Ana was prepared to take. Things were eerily quiet between them since he dislocated her shoulder over a ridiculous television program. Robert hadn't cared for Ana's mood lately and warned her that she was on thin ice. She supposed she could count herself lucky; Robert hadn't killed her yet; though his threats were a daily reminder of how far he would go. Despite regular medication, the effects on Robert were minimal at best. Robert learned how to manipulate the residents and worst of all he was able to manipulate Dr. Lieon.

Ana wished she could be free, free of Robert and the others. In order for that to occur she needed to convince Dr. Lieon that she was well again. Dr. Lieon began treating Ana upon her arrival to Sox a few years ago. In the past year Dr. Lieon often commented on how much progress Ana made, especially in group. The sessions were intimate. The group would sit in a circle and fanaticize about what they would do once they finally left Sox. Ana wasn't like the others, she was aware that she needed help from time to time. She was aware of her differences. There was that time when she was six and her mother beat her so badly, because she was different; not like the other little girls, that her skin became infected from the lashes. She tried to explain to mother that Robert wouldn't allow her to heal, which only made things worse. Mother never blamed Robert for anything, and he took full advantage every opportunity he was given to make Ana's life hell. Their father on the other hand adored Ana. He would tell her how beautiful she was and that she was his special girl. Most of Ana's memories were of her and Robert. He hadn't always been so mean. There was a time briefly where Ana was his protector. The older Robert became the more he seemed to despise her. He would never admit it but she knew that he blames her for their being at Sox. But there was no time to worry about that now. It was time for bed.

Ana lifted her weary body from the small wooden chair that sat by the window. The years of wear shown on the brown wood as it peeked through the dinged white paint. She scurried across the cold blue tile floor taking great care not to make noise. Robert was asleep and there would be hell to pay if he awoke. As Ana laid there with the covers pulled tight up under her chin she tried to remember what Dr. Lieon told her.

"If you see something bad, close your eyes and tell yourself it's not real three times and when you open them again, it will be gone."

It was late and Ana was concerned because Dr. Lieon was never late for her nightly visits. Ana had become Dr. Lieon's favorite patient and it was obvious. The others were jealous and often isolated Ana when Dr. Lieon was not around. It wasn't like the doctor not to check in and say goodnight. Her concern slowly melted as she gave way to the warm feeling of the medicine and her eyes grew heavier as she began to drift off. Ana was almost asleep when she felt something covering her mouth and nose. She was pinned to the bed. She tried to open her eyes, but the room was dark. The moonlight did little to help Ana who was struggling to free herself. Ana quickly closed her eyes. She could still hear Robert breathing, he was asleep and she needed his help.

As Ana fought to get free, she remembered Dr. Lieon's words and began to say in her mind it's not real, it's not real, it's not real, but it was. Tears formed in the corner of Ana's eyes as Ana, along with the covers from her bed, were flung to the floor. The pain was more than she could take. Her dislocated shoulder was now broken. Her fall awoke Robert who was now furious. Ana scooted closer to the bed and could see Robert quickly approaching. His fist met Ana's flesh as the door to room closed. It had been one of the others, but Robert didn't see them. Just like Mother, no matter what Ana said he wouldn't believe her. She needed Dr. Lieon now more than ever.

~ 1 ~

Three years of Emalee's life was dedicated to her research and she could now see the light at the end of the tunnel. The long days of reviewing articles and journals would now be a thing of the past. She could now return her focus to treating her patients. For every night she spent walking the whispering halls of Sox, she came one step closer on her journey to become the Department Lead. Emalee witnessed various stages of psychosis with her patients and her research was ground breaking. Allison Whitman, the Department Chair at Sox's Research Hospital for the Mentally Insane was Emalee's toughest critic, and a tough pill to swallow. Allison's habit of constantly probing Emalee annoyed her to no end. Her line of questioning made Emalee feel minuscule. Allison was not one to accept that research hadn't found the answer to a particular question. They were doctors, they were researchers, and there was a logical explanation for everything. Emalee sat in her office compiling the last of the information to be reviewed. With any luck she would be able to convince the board to sponsor her continued research on MPD, Multiple Personality Disorder. As she placed her research in the binder, Allison walked into her office.

"Just the person I needed to see.

"Me?" Allison asked looking out Emalee's office window.

Allison do you mind reviewing this?"

Emalee handed over her life's work with both excitement and fear. Would Allison think it was any good she wondered? Emalee's nomination for supervising department lead would all come down to this research. She rang her fingers as she awaited Allison's response. The room was quiet, almost too quiet as Emalee took short deep breaths. She could feel the sweat as it puddled underneath her arms. Emalee bit at the skin around her nail bed as she tried to decipher Allison's expressions.

Allison took the papers and flipped through them, not seemingly interested in any particular section. She glanced at Emalee a few times with a blank expression that was hard for Emalee to interpret. Allison's strawberry blonde eyebrows furrowed as she read through Emalee's work.

"Interesting." Was all that Allison said.

"What's interesting Allison?"

"Your view, especially when you say *The Others* are located within a person's subconscious and are indeed viable and necessary to an individual's psyche."

Allison began to walk the room as she continued to read Emalee's work aloud. The sound of her heels against the wood floor reminded Emalee of a judge striking their gavel in judgment.

"They reside in a place known as the shadows where repressed personalities are completely unaware of each other. Most of us are unware that the others exist as they only appear under and through deep psychological stimulation. *The Others* are what the psyche believes they are.

"Emalee this is absolutely astounding."

Emalee exhaled the breath she held and began to straighten the disarray of papers and journals that covered her desk.

"So Emalee are you making any progress with your patients?"

Emalee looked up from under her eyes at Allison who placed her research on the edge of the desk.

"What to do you mean by progress? You know as well as I do most of them are lifers. I do all I can to normalize them, but many will never fit into society."

Allison slammed her hand against the papers, which caused Emalee to jump, knocking several journals to the floor.

"Then I guess you have failed them."

Allison turned her back and began to gather her belongings. As she placed a tan coat over her arm, she turned to Emalee.

"I did have such high hopes for you."

Emalee rushed from the desk hoping she could say something to persuade Allison.

"Allison wait, what about the department lead position?"

Allison smiled snidely.

"You need not concern yourself with that."

Emalee slowly closed the door to her office, she felt deflated. *What am I going to do now?* She thought to herself. Thousands of hours of planning and researching would go unrewarded. Allison didn't seem to care about the many years and tears she'd spent compiling the information. Now it was all for not, it would go unnoticed much like Emalee over the past few years. There was a chime and the strong aroma of coffee filled the air. It was two o'clock. Emalee's Keurig began perking her favorite afternoon delight. She desperately needed something to pick her spirits up. There were a million things to do before her shift at Sox began. Emalee carefully sipped on the hazelnut coffee taking care not to burn her lip. Her mind ran through the list of things she needed to do. Consumed with finishing her research, she missed a few nights with Ana. Ana was never far from her mind. It seemed like the more progress Ana made the tighter Robert's grip became on her. There was something about Ana that Emalee felt genuinely connected to. Emalee wanted more than anything for Ana to be well enough to leave Sox and it appeared she might get her wish soon. Ana showed great improvement over the past few months. Though she held back in group, she became more determine to break her dependence on Robert.

Robert on the other hand was months if not years away from being ready to reenter society. His violent outburst and uncountable nature not only frightened Ana, but made Emalee feel unnerved in their sessions. His eyes were often glazed over and when he did make direct eye contact; Emalee felt naked and violated. There was something in the way he smiled that rattled her core. It was never a smile of happiness, more like a smirk where he was the keeper of a dark secret. Research proved that children were often imprinted on differently, despite growing up in the same home. And it wasn't uncommon for siblings to share similar physiological anatomies. Both shared the same environmental stimuli, but it was their unique responses that puzzled Emalee.

At the onset of their treatment Emalee believed Ana held repressed memories of her childhood, while

Robert replayed the events daily. It was the only way to explain their varied outlooks on life. Emalee thought Robert suffered a larger chemical imbalance, which would explain his rash behavior. There was no shortage of intelligence in either Robert or Ana as they both scored right at genius level on multiple aptitude tests.

Emalee adjusted the blinds of her office window and gazed down onto the courtyard below. Several orderlies and patients were amidst the grounds of Sox. A breeze emitted from the thin panes of the glass that were in desperate need of repair. Emalee struggled to adjust to the severity of the patients at the research facility. There was nothing quite as terrifying as being in a room with a patient that hadn't shown any remorse for their actions. Even worse were those that held a disregard for the human life. Emalee wasn't intimidated by them; she was intrigued by their differences. She wanted to know more about what made them tick and the things that seemed to trigger their episodes and outbursts. By the time Emalee completed her third year at the facility, she became accustomed to the challenges of dealing with mental patients. As with every challenge Emalee managed to see her way through, though she was not without her own demons.

Emalee continued to gaze out of the window. The autumn leaves added flecks of orange and red to the dying grass below. She remembered how she loved fall and the way her father would rake the leaves in to a pile in the front yard for her to play in. But that was all a distant memory, only one of the few she still had of her father. She was so young when he passed; all that remained were photos to remember his face. Emalee remembered everything about the day of her father's death. The house smelt of oak, as the ashes glittered in the fire place. It was time for bed and she'd spent half an hour looking around the house for him. For as long as she could remember her father would chase her around the room before bedtime and place a red fire engine beside her. He would tell her fantastical stories and there was always a fireman like her father to the rescue. That night however, he did not come into her room. With the fire engine in her hand Emalee turned the door knob and pushed open the door to the study. Her father sat behind an old wooden desk. The fire crackled in the background and the overhead light was off. Her father sat at the antique desk with the dim light of the lonely bulb barely illuminating the room. The ambient light left the room in shadows and Emalee felt afraid; there was something wrong with her father, he never slept in the study. His posture was slumped in the chair and he didn't move when she entered the room.

In a light voice Emalee called out from the doorway but father didn't respond. She moved a step closer and squinted as her young eyes tried to make out her father's expression. Her heart raced; father was known for scaring her, and she anticipated him jumping at any moment, only to tickle her to the floor. As she got closer she could see an angry cut slashed down the side of his face onto his neck. There was a trail of dark blood from his hairline to his chest. His eyes were open and they stared right at her. Emalee tapped on her father's arm as she whispered, only to have his arms fall to his side before hitting the floor. The sound of his lifeless body as it struck the hardwood floors caused her to drop the fire engine as she screamed. Mother quickly appeared as Emalee stood frozen next to her father. No words were exchanged as mother took Emalee by the arm along with the fire engine up to Emalee's room. Each step felt like it was miles away from her room, but not far enough. There Emalee laid with the covers tucked in all around her as her mother placed the fire engine on the nightstand. Emalee could feel the warmth from her mother's body through the covers as she laid there sobbing. Mother gently brushed the hairs away from her face and told her.

"If you see something bad, close your eyes and tell yourself it's not real three times and when you open them again, it will be gone."

There they laid together in silence until Emalee fell asleep. In the morning when Emalee awoke, she ran down the stairs hoping it was all a bad dream. The door to the study was open and on the desk sat her fire engine. She searched throughout the house, opening every door, every closet before heading to the garage. Father's car was there and cold. Mother's car was in the yard but they were nowhere to be found. Emalee was alone. It was all just a bad dream Emalee thought as she smiled to herself. Emalee headed back into the house and once in the kitchen she pulled a stool up to the counter. She made herself a bowl of cereal before returning to the study. Emalee greedily ate her cereal; as she played with her fire engine on the floor. She knew that at any minute mother and father would be in and her day would begin. As she ate her last bite, the engine rolled across the study floor and stopped at the edge of the wooden desk. She scooted across the dusty floor, which was in much need of sweeping and reached for the engine. She picked the engine up and noticed something on the wheels. Emalee took her fingers and wiped the wheel before putting her finger in her mouth. The taste was metallic and bitter. Emalee didn't like the taste but it was familiar.

Emalee didn't like thinking about her past, in fact she did all she could to avoid it, as much of it as possible. She took the last sip of her coffee as she glanced at the clock. It was now a quarter to three and time for her to make her rounds. She grabbed her coat from the back of her chair and hurried out of her office. It would take her the entire fifteen minutes to make it across the courtyard and through security if she went by foot.

Luckily there was a golf cart nearby which would aid her efforts to keep to her schedule. Emalee was good about being on time; she needed to be, many of her patients experienced anxieties and fears and being late would only exasperate matters.

As soon as Emalee entered the ward she was met with excitement. She barely made it through the doors when she found out that a sedative was administered to Robert. Emalee looked at Robert on the gurney and felt pity for him. He was peaceful in comparison to his normally aggressive nature. Robert was six feet tall with broad shoulders. His hair was dark auburn in stark contrast to Ana's winter wheat. His eyes were a cold green and seemed to take in everything. There was a scar just above his right eye in the shape of a C. Sedated and restrained Robert wasn't any more threating than a butterfly.

"What happened here? Why is the patient being transported?"

A thin bottled red head looked up from behind the computer screen.

"That man there is my patient, why is he being transported?"

The redhead looked confused as she flipped through several charts before shrugging her shoulders.

"I am Dr. Lieon. Dr. Emalee Lieon. That is my patient Robert Morrison, why is he being moved?"

"Oh Dr. Lieon, they tried to call you."

"They who?"

Emalee grew increasingly more agitated with the receptionist who appeared more concerned with filing her nails than answering Emalee.

"I guess one of the doctors. Mr. Morrison had an episode last night and broke his roommates shoulder, or something like that. When they couldn't reach you; the on-call placed orders for him to be moved to solitary."

The red head's accent was thick; she was definitely not a local. Her round face and freckles reminded Emalee of a raggedy Ann doll.

"Where is Ana?"

"Who?"

"Ana Morrison, the patient's roommate?"

Where did they get these people from? She wasn't qualified to watch a rock, much less patients. Emalee thought to herself.

"Oh, she is in her room."

Emalee hurried down the hall to check on Ana. Emalee was so consumed with her research she'd neglected to focus on what was important, her patients. Emalee lightly knocked on the door before entering. Ana laid on her side atop the covers. Emalee could see that Ana's arm and shoulder were casted. Emalee immediately felt guilty as she drew nearer. She pulled up a chair and sat near the window as she couldn't bear to look at Ana.

"Ana" she whispered softly. Though her face was swollen, she could tell that Ana was awake. Ana's smooth peach skin was now spotted with hues of red, blue and purple. Emalee saw traces of dried blood crusted on her lips.

"Why don't we get you cleaned up; that will make you feel better." Emalee wanted to keep her tone light as she tried to hide her own regret.

"Go away." Ana said in the smallest voice.

"Ana, I am here to help you."

Emalee moved closer to Ana who closed her eyes.

"I waited all night for you Dr. Lieon and you never came."

"But Ana I am here now."

Just as Emalee finished her sentence, the receptionist spoke over the p.a. system. "Dr. Lieon; paging Dr. Lieon.

~2~

malee hated to leave Ana in such a vulnerable state, but she was being paged by the annoying redhead up front. Emalee watched Ana, who by this time had covered her head with a handmade blanket. Emalee saw there were scratches in the window sill as she turned away. She took note to ask Ana about that upon her return. Emalee made her way down the drab gray sterile halls of Sox before reaching the front desk. The redhead didn't hear Emalee approach and jumped when she tapped on the counter.

"You paged Dr. Lieon?"

"Yes. You are needed in the assessment room."

Emalee turned away from the counter feeling annoyed about her and Ana being interrupted. There were other resident's available to assess a patient. She'd forgotten to grab a clipboard and note pad before leaving the front desk which only added to her frustration. As she rounded the corner to the assessment room, Emalee passed Johnathan, the video tech in the hall. All sessions with clients were record as standard procedure for Sox.

"Hey where are going, isn't there a patient in there?" Emalee asked.

Johnathan smiled a big smile and nodded.

"Oh hello Dr. Lieon; yes he is in there. I just need to grab a quick cup of coffee. Don't worry; I already have the session recording and ready for you."

Johnathan was off and down the hall before she could respond. Emalee opened the door to the AV room and hoped to find a pen and a notebook located under the mess of Johnathan's discarded potato chip bags. Through the one way mirror in the AV room, Emalee could see a figure standing in front of the pictures. Though Emalee could not make out his age, she could see that his back was curved and his shoulders were uneven. The patient appeared calm at the moment, but there was no way for Emalee to know what she was walking into. The patient was small in stature, almost frail to her. As Emalee exited the AV room, she wondered what secrets he would reveal if any. She glanced down the hall to see if Johnathan had return, but the halls were empty and quiet. She entered the assessment room with an expressionless face; she wanted to remain in control. The room consisted of a couch, a heavy wooden chair and abstract art that were securely mounted to the walls. In Emalee's haste to get to get to the room, she neglected to obtain the patient's file.

"Hello I am Dr. Lieon." She said as she closed the door to the room.

The patient sat quietly in a wooden chair with his gaze affixed on a black and white zig zag painting.

"I will ask you a few questions if that's ok?"

The patient continued to stare at the painting.

"Do you mind telling me your name?"

Emalee noticed the patient wincing but he remained nonverbal. She sat on the far corner of the couch where she could keep an eye on the patient. Emalee made herself comfortable on the couch and removed her coat as she began to take notes.

"Well then, I will begin by telling you a little about myself. As I mention before I am Dr. Lieon, Senior Resident here at Sox."

The patient continued to stare at the lines on the painting, as he spoke.

"I like your scarf."

Emalee was stunned. With all the excitement upon her arrival she'd forgotten that she was wearing her scarf. She wondered how he noticed as he never looked at her directly.

"Thank you." She stammered. Emalee was perplexed by the slowness of his speech. She wondered if he the patient was medicated; which would mean she didn't have much time to speak with him before the effects of the medication took hold.

"As I said, I am the senior resident here so you are in good hands."

The patient dropped his head and spoke slowly.

"My mother use to wear scarfs."

His words were forced as he spoke more to the floor than Emalee.

"Would you like to talk about your mother, what was she like?"

Emalee felt it was a good sign that the patient was about to open up to her. Talking about his mother would give her some sort of insight to what she was about to deal with. The patient didn't respond, he lifted his head and began starring at the picture once again.

"I see that you like that picture."

Emalee changed her line of questioning; maybe it was too soon to inquire about the patient's mother. Without knowing his history, she didn't want to do anything to shut the patient down before she could make any headway. Emalee sought to obtain as much information from him as she could. She needed him to trust her; it would be easier for her to get a feel for his psychosis if his wasn't guarded.

"I also enjoy that one." Emalee said. "Does the picture make you think of anything in particular?"

Emalee took notice of the distinct curvature of his spine; she suspected the early onset of scoliosis.

"Does the picture make you feel anything?"

"Hot," was the patient's reply. His comment struck Emalee as odd as she jotted a few notes on her pad. She noted that the patient was very rigid and guarded. Emalee couldn't tell if it was the patient's nature to be so closed off or if it was due to the fact that she was a woman.

"Let's talk about it. Do you feel anything else?"

Emalee thought it best to keep the patient talking for as long as possible. She couldn't wait to review the video to pick up on anything she might have missed in the session.

"I want it to stop!"

The patient blurted out of nowhere causing Emalee to drop her pen. She kept her gazed locked as she reached down to pick up her pen.

"What do you want to stop?

Emalee became excited at the idea of finally making headway with the patient. She quickly scribbled on the note pad and stopped when she saw the patient turn. This was the first time she was able to take a good look at the mystery man. He appeared to be in his early forties, no facial hair or distinguishing features. He was a thin lipped man with dark brown beady eyes. His hair was tossed and he wore a thin dress shirt and slacks. As her eyes made their way down, she saw that zip ties bound his wrist. He sat in the chair barefoot staring straight ahead.

"What is it that you want to stop?

He slowly looked down towards his lap. He lifted his hands and Emalee could see that he was fully erect. She took stock of her outfit; she always made sure never to wear anything that would accentuate her figure. There was nothing stimulating about the black clogs which adorned her feet. They were made even more unattractive by the fact that Emalee's feet were larger than most women. The only thing out of place with her basic medical attire was her scarf. It was a blue and green flowered scarf which she purchased several years ago. It was faded and showed signs of wear with its frayed ends. Emalee paused for a moment before she spoke again. She crafted her words careful.

"Does that occur often, your excitement I mean?"

The patient quickly turned back to the wall of art, but this time he did not look at the painting that held his attention for most of the session. She hadn't meant to embarrass him with her question and she now wished that she asked something different away from the subject. The patient spoke in almost an inaudible tone.

"It only happens when I see scarfs. I like scarfs."

"Tell me about that."

As if someone flipped a switch, the frail man sat up straight in the chair. He began to speak in third person as he told his story. The florescent lighting of the room danced off the creases of his face as he transformed into a more animated figure.

"He didn't want to, but he had no choice. He took the scarf from the dresser drawer, where she kept it. He waited for her to become distracted, she was looking for her keys. He quickly placed the scarf up to her mouth so she couldn't scream. He could feel his adrenaline racing. He moved the coffee table with his foot as he struggled to get her to the floor. He pinned her arms with his knees as he struck the back of her head against the floor. It was enough to daze her. Her eyes once bright hung low. He took great care not to mark her body any more than necessary. Her milky white skin excited him. He carefully removed her clothing as she laid half-conscious on the floor. He took his time in unbuttoning his dress shirt."

As the patient recanted the story, Emalee could see that his body and posture were that of a much younger and stronger man. He was no longer the feeble middle age man; she found when she entered the room. He became excited as the words that were once forced now flowed freely. Emalee wanted to know who or what exactly was he describing, so she let him continue without interruption.

"He folded his shirt neatly as it was heavily starched; and wrinkles annoyed him. She was groggy but still alive when he took her. He could feel her flesh peel back as he forced his way. Her eyes bugged from the pain and quickly closed. He pulled the scarf tighter around her neck as her body fought for air; he went quicker than he hoped. He grabbed the tail ends of the scarf and pulled tightly as he expelled himself. He felt a release flow through his veins as the skin around her neck turn fire red and the whites of her eyes filled with blood. She looked so peaceful; he couldn't bear to leave her on the floor. He took her lifeless body to the bedroom, where he pulled back the covers and placed her still warm body safely beneath the black and white comforter. He kissed her lips before telling her good night."

Emalee scribbled as fast as she could on the note pad. She wrote so furiously that she etched words on the pages below. Upon reaching the end of the story the patient stood, Emalee could see the retelling of the horrors had been too much for him. He stood in front of the pictures with his shoulders once again hunched over, but this time his pants were soiled with his expression of the tale. He looked up at Emalee like a little child ashamed as he quietly spoke.

"I would like to go home now.

More than ever, Emalee needed to see the patient's file. She wasn't sure if she was dealing with a potential serial killer or a multiple personality disorder. Either way she needed more information. Emalee slowly removed the scarf from her neck and stuffed it in the pocket of her lab coat. Not knowing if the patient would slip into another level of psychosis she grabbed the pen and note pad as the patient turned to stare at the zigzag picture on the wall and left the room. She held the knob as to not disturb the apparent trance the patient was now captive in. Upon entering the AV room she found Johnathan sipping his coffee and eating a bagel.

"Please tell me you have all of that on tape."

Johnathan looked up from his bagel; his headphones were in and hadn't heard her question. He wiped his mouth with the back of his wrist and removed the crumbs that were lodged in the corner of his mouth.

"Did you say something?"

Emalee rolled her eyes in disgust at the fact Johnathan failed to listen in on the session. He would have never known that she was in danger until it was too late.

"Never mind, make a copy of the tape and have it on my desk within the hour."

She demanded as she left the room; Johnathan wondered why Dr. Lieon was so unnerved. She was normally one of the more pleasant doctors at Sox. As Emalee approached the front desk, several of the interns quickly scattered leaving the receptionist clambered for something to say. Emalee stood with her lips pursed together; she could feel her face burn as it became flushed. The redhead receptionist descended slowly into the black mesh back chair.

"Is there anything I can help you with Dr. Lieon?"

Emalee starred at the receptionist with her dark brown eyes as she straightened her posture.

"As a matter of fact there is. Locate the file for the patient in the assessment room." Emalee watched as the redhead rotated her head.

"File, there was no file."

"There has to be a file where did the patient come from?"

"He was already processed in when I came in this morning."

"Well he came from somewhere; he did not appear out of thin air, now find me that file."

Emalee realized she was yelling and felt the eyes of the orderlies burning against her face. It wasn't like her to become unnerved. She needed to get her bearings; Emalee didn't want any of her negative energy to transfer when she saw Ana again. She checked on several patients as she made her rounds through the ward. Once everything was done, Emalee planned to give Ana her full attention before heading off to process intakes for the evening. Robert would be her last visit, as he always altered her mood. Emalee wasn't afraid of Robert; he was more difficult to manage than Ana, which always made things interesting.

As Emalee made her way down the hall she noticed that Ana's room door was ajar. Emalee quickened her steps across the speckled linoleum floor. With each step she felt more and more tense. The patients were never allowed to leave their room unattended. She reached the door and could see that Ana was not in the room. She felt a cool breeze as she entered. Emalee walked over to the window were she could see a small piece of broken glass. She would need to report it immediately. She turned to leave the room but stopped when she saw a small red notebook with black velvet binding on Ana's bed. Emalee picked the notebook up and flipped through several pages. On several pages Ana practiced the things she'd learned in group. Ana jotted down her feelings and the things she needed to stay away from. As Emalee flipped to the middle of the journal she observed something odd, a change in the writing. Maybe Ana was using her left hand, since Robert recently injured her shoulder. Emalee turned the page again and saw only two words were on the page, *The Others*. She continued to flip through the journal and the two words were repeated on every page until she reached the end, where Ana had written so hard that the writing was etched into the back jacket of the journal. ***THE OTHERS.***

~3~

S he carefully placed the journal back on Ana's bed unsure of what to make of her findings. Was Emalee wrong about Ana's progress? Had she been so consumed with her research that she missed the obvious? Ana might be worse than she imagined. Ana only mentioned the others a few times before, though Emalee was still unsure exactly as to whom the others were. The mere fact that the others existed disturbed Emalee, whoever they were. The real question was why were they back and so prominent in Ana's mind? Emalee walked over to Robert's bed which was meticulously made. The bedspread was pulled taught with the pillow erected to form a perfect rectangle across the top of the bed. The side table contained a new charcoal drawing. Emalee stared at the drawing for a few minutes trying to decipher the unusual shapes that stretched across the canvas. The drawing was dark and just as mysterious as Robert. A sudden chill came across her as she focused on what appeared to be eyes on the drawing. The charcoal pencil that was attached to the drawing fell to the floor. Emalee placed the drawing back on the side table as she knelt down to retrieve the pencil from underneath Robert's bed. She felt around in the darkness with her finger tips until she could reach the pencil.

As she withdrew her arm; Emalee felt grooves with her fingertips extending just beyond the edge of the bed. She placed the pencil on the side table, and then she lifted the side of the bed covers to face the darkness. Emalee pulled her phone from her lab coat and used the small beam of light to see. Under the bed she found eight long scratch marks carved into the wood. One of the grooves contained a small beige sliver. Emalee removed the small item from the tracks and realized it was a broken finger nail. The staining of blood on the side meant that it was fresh. Emalee stood taking great care to replace all of Robert's items in the exact order in which she found them. While she was very concerned for Ana's safety, she knew that she needed to meet with Robert first. Against her better judgment she allowed them to be housed together, but she could no longer stand by while Robert expounded his abuse on Ana. Emalee would need to issue orders to have Ana transferred to another room before the night was over to ensure Ana's safety. As she closed the door on the room Emalee had a nagging feeling in the pit of her stomach that things were going to get worse before they would get better.

The afternoon flew by and pains of hunger crept upon Emalee. She headed to the cafeteria where a few other doctors were finishing their meals. The clock on the cafeteria wall read seven o'clock; soon it would be time to hand out medication for the night. She purchased a packet of crackers and a soda from the vending machine before heading off to find Robert. Again she passed Ana's room, the door remained opened. Emalee wondered if Ana was being treated in the infirmary, which would explain her absence. An hour had passed since dinner and there hadn't been a single alarm or siren alerting the staff of any missing patients. By now Ana must have returned to her room as no one was looking for a missing patient. Emalee passed by her office on her way to see Robert and noticed that the light was on. She entered the office wondering if she'd forgotten to turn the light off from the day before, but surely the cleaning crew would have noticed. In the middle of her desk sat a copy of the video from the mystery man's session. Emalee thought it better to wait until she was able to review his file before watching the tape.

As she turned to leave, she heard a faint noise coming from her private bathroom. She proceeded slowly with caution. The bath was dark with only the light from her office showing through. She flipped the switch and the sound stopped. Emalee looked around, but there was nothing there. She turned the light off and closed the door. She began to leave her office when she heard the noise once again. Emalee wasn't mistaken; she walked in the direction of the bathroom but quickly realized the noise was not coming from that direction, but from her desk. Emalee gingerly approached her desk; not knowing what to expect. The noise was low, almost like the growl of a wounded animal. She searched the top of her desk for something to protect herself with. She grabbed a pair of scissors and removed them from the pencil holder. Emalee slid the chair away from her desk and the noise once again stopped. Her heart raced as she stood a few inches away from her desk. She was startled as her phone rang. Emalee heard a sniffle as she got closer to the desk.

"Ana?"

She placed the scissors on the chair and lowered herself onto all fours entering the shadows of her desk. Ana sat with her knees to her chest; though Emalee could not see her face she could tell that she was crying. Emalee moved back and sat on her bottom as she extended her hand toward Ana.

"It's ok Ana; there is no one here that will hurt you." Ana sat motionless under the desk.

"Ana can you hear me, its Dr. Lieon."

Emalee was incensed at the idea that Ana had been left alone. How did anyone not notice her roaming the halls of Sox unescorted? Had no one noticed the petite wheat haired girl with the casted arm?

"I'm cold," Ana said through her tears.

"Come on let's get you from under there."

Emalee wobbled until she could steady herself on her feet. She reached out for Ana, taking great measure to ensure that she did not hit her head as she exited from under the desk. Emalee suspected that Ana must have gone missing sometime after leaving the infirmary, as she was still wearing the standard hospital gown. What were the interns thinking leaving a patient alone? They should have confirmed that her room door was locked. Emalee saw Ana shivering in the full light of the office. Her hair was loose and hung in her face. Ana shared the same green eyes as Robert; however hers were softer and gentler. Emalee scanned her office for anything she could use to wrap Ana in. She saw a small blanket lying on the top of her bookshelf.

"Stay right here Ana, don't move." Emalee went to the shelf to remove the blanket.

"You will have to excuse the dust, but it is all that I have."

Emalee shook the blanket, freeing the dust that collected on the outside folds. She wrapped the blanket around Ana as she took care to be mindful of her arm. As Ana reached to grab the blanket, Emalee saw that her nails were broken and there were remnants of blood on her index finger.

"Are you hungry?

Emalee asked trying to gauge Ana's mood. Ana shook her head.

"Well then let's get you back to your room." Ana's eyes grew wide as she looked at Emalee.

"What's wrong Ana?" Ana backed away from Emalee and held the blanket tightly around her shoulders as she whispered,

"The Others."

Emalee didn't intend to start a session with Ana tonight, however Ana's present state of mind demanded her full attention. She became uneasy at the idea of having her placed in a new room all alone. Emalee motioned for Ana to have seat as she walked to close her office door. Ana sat Indian style in the middle of the ostentatious Persian rug that covered Emalee's floor. Emalee watched as Ana's eyes darted back and forth while rocking. She had never witnessed Ana display behavior such as this, and thought for a moment it may have been better if this was being recorded. But there was no time for that. Emalee pulled a chair from the corner of the room and placed it in the middle of the floor in front of Ana. She sat quietly for a moment watching Ana who seemed unaware that she was being observed. It was completely out to the ordinary for her to have a patient in her office, in fact Emalee was sure that it was against policy, but she continued.

"So tell me Ana, when did *The Others* return?"

Emalee hoped she would be able to link the return of the faceless *Others* with a particular event which would explain their existence. She believed Ana created *The Others* as a way to project any misgiving away from her-self.

"They have always been here Dr. Lieon." Ana's voice was cold and matter of fact, in comparison to her normal sheepish tone.

"Where are they now?"

"They are in here with us."

"Can you see them Ana?"

"Yes, can't you."

"No Ana, I can't. Maybe they don't want to reveal themselves to me."

Emalee saw that Ana became agitated by her statement.

"You are just like Robert and Mother, you don't believe me."

"I do. I do believe *The Others* are real to you Ana, I just can't see them."

"Do you want to see them Dr. Lieon?"

"What do you mean Ana?'

"I can get them to show themselves to you, just close your eyes."

What was Ana up to; was this some sort of trick or mind game Emalee thought. This was strange even for Ana. She still needed to get to the bottom of what happen last night between her and Robert and here Ana wanted to play some sort of game.

"Ok Ana if I agree to close my eyes will *The Others* appear?"

"Yes Dr. Lieon, you just have to believe."

"Ok fine, I believe."

Emalee partially closed her eyes to play along with the hopes that she would soon be able to get to the bottom of everything. Emalee slowly opened one eye and saw Ana still sitting on the floor, but she was now smiling.

"No peeking Dr. Lieon."

"Ok Ana," she sighed. "I will only keep my eyes closed for three more seconds and that's all."

"That is more than enough time Dr. Lieon."

Emalee could hear movement in the room and before she could open her eyes she felt a hand on her shoulder and jumped, Dr. Allison was standing beside her.

"I see this place is getting to you huh?"

"Wait, where is Ana?"

"What do you mean, why would Ana be in your office? You know patients aren't allowed on this side of the campus."

Emalee looked around the room and saw that she was in her main office at Sox, but how.

"Earth to Emalee, I just stopped by to tell you I found your research interesting and will be speaking to the board soon about the Department Lead position."

"Thank you." Emalee said touching her desk and herself as she looked around her office.

"Are you sure you are ok, you look like you could use a good night's rest."

"Maybe you are right, I could use some rest."

Emalee said, halfheartedly as Allison walked out of the office. Emalee was confused, how was it that she was back in her office. She rose from her desk and began to walk to the window when she saw a small note on the floor. It was a yellow sticky and on it written with a charcoal pencil were the words *The Others* in Ana's handwriting. Emalee balled up the sticky and threw it in the trash. She didn't have time for this; someone was obviously playing games.

~4~

Emalee was agitated as she looked at the clock on the wall, it was a quarter to three. She had patients to treat, but in the back of her mind she wondered, had she dreamt it all. There was no way that was possible. She'd been working long hours and focusing on her research, and she didn't know what to think. She grabbed her lab coat and began to button it up when she noticed the blue scarf around her neck. She ran her fingers along the scarf before removing it and placing it on the coat rack. Better safe than sorry she thought as she walked down the hall. Emalee took her time walking across the courtyard, she hated being late, but she needed the time to herself. Her mind was jumbled with her thoughts as they spun around in her head. Emalee needed those few minutes to figure out what was going on with her. She paced herself as the crisp fall air bit at her cheeks. She made sure to stay on the sidewalk, as she hated when her shoes became dirty. The ground was still damp from last night's rain. She waved at a few interns and orderlies as she crossed the courtyard. She could see security off in the distance as she made it to the front door of the housing unit at Sox. The drab gray walls of Sox welcomed her. The halls were eerily quiet and the receptionist was missing from the front desk. Emalee continued to her office, she entered slowly and paused to see if she heard any sounds before turning on the light. All was quiet, she went to her desk and pulled back the chair, there was nothing there besides an old pair of crocs, which she meant to discard some time ago.

Emalee longed to be at ease with the idea that it all had been some sort of dream, but she was now perplexed. With everything going on she thought maybe she was experiencing some sort of mental panic herself, which caused her mind to play tricks on her. She tabled those thoughts for later as she had work to do. There was a small stack of patient files on the corner of her desk. Emalee absolutely adored her desk; innate carvings were etched on the drawers and reminded her of something, though she could never think of what exactly. She often found herself daydreaming as her fingers traced over the indentations in the wood.

As she sat down in her chair Emalee noted a mark on the calendar, today was the anniversary of her father's death. Emalee sank down in her chair as a feeling of guilt began to overwhelm her. She was just a little girl, what could she have done. Though she was able to rationalize in her mind that she had been powerless to help her father, it did nothing to ease the feeling. A tear ran down her left cheek. Her heart wanted nothing more than to be a little child, happy and carefree, but the harsh reality was that she was a child no more. The loud ring of the phone jolted Emalee away from her thoughts and she sat up quickly to answer.

"Hello, this is Dr. Lieon."

It was the redhead, calling to advise that there someone waiting up front. Emalee checked her face in the small compact that lay on her desk. The mirror was cracked, but she hadn't bothered replacing it. She couldn't, it was the only thing she had to remind her of her mother. She could see that her eyes had begun to turn red from her tears. She reached in her drawer to grab her eye drops, but found the small fire engine instead. Emalee held the engine in her hand; she wound the ladder and took a moment to push the toy across her desk. Emalee would have to meet her visitor with a pale face and reddened eyes, despite the momentary joy she received from finding the engine.

Twice a week Emalee would see patients that were considering self-committing to Sox. Most were not in need of the extensive treatment that Sox gave, but on rare occasions she would come across a case so interesting that she and the other department chairs could not afford to let a potential patient go. Ed White was one of those cases. Ed was a fascinating man; he was very well spoken and well-traveled. He much like Emalee lost his parents at an early age, and had not fully come to terms with the lost. Upon their initial meeting Emalee felt there was nothing that she could do to assist Ed. While he did suffer from depression, she thought he would be better suited for traditional therapy until he began to share his visions.

Emalee reached the lobby where Ed waited; he stared out of the lobby window. He was comfortably dressed. He was an average looking gentleman except for his eyes, otherwise he could easily get lost in a crowd.

"Good Afternoon, Ed." Emalee said with a smile.

"Is it? Ed's tone was crass.

"A bit cool, but still lovely none the less," she replied.

It took Emalee sometime to get use to looking at Ed, as he possessed one dark brown eye and one dazzling emerald green eye. She learned to divert her attention during their sessions to avoid making him feel uncomfortable.

"Well I am glad to see you; follow me back to my office."

Emalee caught the receptionist looking up from under her eyes as she and Ed made their way down the hall.

"Good Afternoon Dr. Lieon," she said.

Emalee gave a stern glare as she departed, there was something about her Emalee didn't care for. As if reading her mind Ed spoke.

"If you are going to hire someone to work in a mental institution, at least make sure their voice is not grating."

His tone was harsh but honest. Emalee watched Ed as he walked down the hall and noticed that one of his shoulders was noticeably lower than the other. She hadn't remembered seeing that before, a birth defect perhaps. Ed pushed through the heavy metal doors that separated the lobby from the gray walls of the facility. Emalee's office was one of the few located on the first floor. As they entered her office, Emalee walked over to her desk cutting on the lamp. The sun was beginning to set and the lamp provided a warm glow that many found soothing.

"Tell me Ed, how have things being going for you lately?"

Ed sat in the chair opposite Dr. Lieon. His eyes were slated downward as he plucked at a ball on her Newton's Cradle. It often irritated Emalee when people touched her things, but Ed was different. She began removing the medical journals from her desk as her questioning began.

"Well doc, they have been going."

"How is work?" she asked puzzled by his contrived answer.

"I put on my fake and joyful mask and make due, isn't that what it's all about?" He asked looking directly at Emalee.

"Tell me more about it."

Ed slammed his hand on the desk hard causing Emalee's fire engine to roll from one side to the other.

"I don't need another psychologist meddling inside my brain!"

Emalee was a psychiatrist but now was not the time to explain the difference.

"That is not why you are here Edward."

Her calling his full name was the display of power she needed in order to regain control of the session.

"I don't need another psych evaluation," he mumbled.

"I have been seeing you for eight sessions a month for the past three years; we are well beyond the evaluation stage." She said.

Ed sat back in the burgundy office chair, looking a little more relaxed.

"I'm not crazy you know."

"I hope I never implied that you were; we all need a little help from time to time. That is what I am here for, to help you Ed."

She could see that his raised brows were affixed on the toy engine. Emalee began to remove the engine from her desk when Ed grabbed her wrist.

"Edward you are hurting me."

He released his grip on her wrist, and left behind the prints of his wide fingers on her pale wrist. She quickly put away the engine and repositioned her chair closer to the panic button that was wired inside her desk. Never before had he been aggressive or so flippant in his manners. Something was off with him and she couldn't quite make out what it was. Her pocket buzzed with her alarm. Seven o'clock already. Emalee silenced her alarm as she felt around in her pocket for the small black pouch.

Emalee excused herself from the desk as she walked over to her private restroom. She kept Ed in view as she filled a small glass with water. She removed the round white pill from the pouch and placed it under her tongue. She almost choked as she glanced at Ed's empty chair. The glass shattered as it fell into the small white porcelain sink.

"Edward!" she called out as she exited the tiny room. She was startled by the heavy wooden door closing being behind her. Edward stood in front of the bookshelf and smiled as he held picture of her father.

"You know you look a lot like your father."

"Thank you, but I never said that was my father."

"Oh I assumed he would be; you have the same jaw line and the same cleft chin."

A familiar nagging feeling returned to the pit of her stomach as she stood to the side of her desk.

"Ed, let's continue our session. Please have a seat."

Ed placed the picture frame back on the shelf, taking time to reposition it in its exact spot before facing Dr. Lieon. Ed smiled at Dr. Lieon and she in kind gave a warm smile. Her smile faded as Edward's face shifted.

"You must take me for a fool Dr. Lieon."

Emalee moved closer to the panic button as Ed approached.

"What are you talking about Edward?"

"You are just as crazy as I am; aren't you?"

"Edward you're not crazy and neither am I" she said as her words cracked.

"I saw you take those pills Doc."

"Oh, I take medicine twice a day for migraines; I've had them since I was a child."

Ed slowly walked back to the chair and stood in front of the desk. He gave Emalee a once over, and his eyes seemed to respond separately and jointly at the same time. Emalee waited to see if Ed had regained his senses.

"Migraines you say?" Ed stared at Emalee as though he didn't believe her given explanation.

"Yes migraines. Honestly Edward, I wouldn't be able to treat you if I suffered from any psychosis. I assure you everything is fine. I'm fine."

Emalee forced the corners of her mouth into a smile.

"Migraines... are you sure you don't have black outs?"

Emalee was puzzled as to his line of questioning. He was the patient that sought out Sox for treatment and he now wanted to play the role of psychiatrist.

"Edward, I assure you it is nothing more than the occasional migraine. Millions of people suffer from them and take medication to manage them. Nothing more, now please have a seat."

Emalee gestured for Ed to sit, but he stood just starring at her with those eyes.

"You really don't remember do you Dr. Lieon?'

"Edward, I apologize, I don't follow you. Please have a seat and we can discuss this further."

Edward stood in front of the desk and slowly moved his head from side to side. Emalee could hear the bones in his neck as they popped.

"Edward please have a seat; you are frightening me."

Ed gave a haughty laugh as he continued to stare.

"It isn't you who should be afraid of me, I should be afraid of you."

"Why would you have to fear me?" Emalee asked as she watched her patient slip into a fit of madness before her eyes.

"Because you want to fix me, change me."

"I only want to help you, isn't that why you came here?"

"No Dr. Lieon that is why you called me here."

Emalee stood there looking at Edward. If she wasn't sure before, she was more than positive now that Edward needed ongoing treatment. She felt that in his current state he would not voluntarily admit himself. Emalee inched her fingers over the carvings toward the panic button. Suddenly she was at a loss for air as Edward held the collar of her lab coat in his hand. He pulled her close and her feet lifted from the floor. She could feel the hard wood of her desk pressing against her stomach and legs as she frantically tried to reach the panic button.

"Let's see if you remember now."

Ed said as he gripped the collar of her coat tighter. Emalee could feel the life draining from her body as she looked into his two miss colored eyes. She saw a faint smile come across his lips as she faded away. Her eyes went dim and she could hear her mother's voice in her ear saying,

"If you see something bad, close your eyes and tell yourself it's not real three times and when you open them again, it will be gone."

~5~

Ana woke to the sound of rain beating against her window. Robert's bed was empty. She looked around the room, and she was alone. She felt a release of tension from her body like a helium balloon floating in the air. She felt weightless; all of her sadness was temporarily suspended. She laid there blotting away the tears with her hand as sheets of rain fell. Ana kicked off her covers to peer outside the window. The bite of the air ran through her gown. As the storm grew louder, Ana grew more afraid. She had always been afraid of storms. The lights of the courtyard came one by one as the clouds rolled. To Ana it appeared the sky was filled with oil and spilling over everything. What a funny thing she thought, now why on earth would there be oil in the sky. She quickly ran away from the window as a streak of lighting illuminated her room. Ana hated being left alone with Robert but she hated being alone during a storm more. When she was younger she would often stow away in Robert's room until the storm passed. Robert never allowed her in his bed, despite her crying. He would threaten to tell Mother if Ana didn't stop all her whining. But she was alone. Ana's fleeting moments of happiness gave way as the storm approached full on. The loud claps of thunder were enough to stop her heart. Ana returned to her bed and pulled the covers tightly around her head. She wanted to blot out the storm, but the lightening cut through the covers. Ana feared lightening even more than she did the roars of the thunder. She would often attribute the harsh sound of thunder to a herd of elephants traveling across the sky, but the lightening, the lightening terrified her. It was during the lightening that the faces of *The Others* would appear. Ana closed her eyes tightly and counted One Mississippi, Two Mississippi as she prepared herself for the next clap of thunder. There was a hard knock on the door and Ana released a wail.

"Ana calm down it's me Dr. Allison."

Ana slowly removed the covers from her head. She was puzzled to see Dr. Allison. It was not often that she saw her, and when she did, Ana often wished she hadn't. Dr. Allison was cold like mother and Ana could never seem to provide the answers that she was looking for.

"Where is Dr. Lieon?" Ana asked sheepishly.

"I was hoping that you could tell me," she said while closing the door behind her.

"Going to bed so soon Ana? It's only eight o'clock."

Ana hated the sound of Dr. Allison's voice, she always spoke so slowly. Ana hated the way she made her feel. There was no way for Ana to know what time it was. The room was almost dark. The sky was without a moon and a few of the lights that lit the path of the courtyard had been damaged by the storm. Dr. Allison thrust the room into brightness by flipping on the overhead lights. It caused Ana to squint at the rush of light which invaded her eyes.

Dr. Allison methodically walked around the room; she stopped for a few moments at the foot of Robert's bed before making her way over to the nightstand where she began to remove the drawing. Ana sat upright in the bed.

"Don't touch that!" she blurted out.

"Why not?"

Dr. Allison asked without turning to face Ana.

"Because he will know, he'll think that I did it."

"And that concerns you, doesn't it Ana?

Ana didn't reply as they both knew the answer. Dr. Allison removed her hands and placed them in the pockets of her lab coat before facing Ana.

"Have you seen your precious Dr. Lieon?

Ana dropped her head as she shook it from side to side. She wondered where Dr. Lieon had gone off to. It had been a few days, maybe even a week, Ana wasn't sure of how long it had been since she'd seen Dr. Lieon. She only knew that she needed her. *The Others* and Robert wouldn't allow her a moment's peace and with her arm injured she was unable to protect herself from either of them.

"Well if she does stop by your room, let her know that I am looking for her, can you do that?'

Ana nodded as she watch Dr. Allison walk to the door.

"Oh and Ana, I do hope that you have sweet dreams."

Dr. Allison closed the door; and Ana was relieved that she was finally gone. She glanced at the door and could see Dr. Allison frame still standing there; she could hear voices but couldn't make out who she was speaking to. As Ana gazed upon the narrow rectangle glass in the door she thought she saw Dr. Allison and one of *The Others* smiling directly at her.

~6~

The ticking of the metronome on the small table lulled Robert further into the darkness. Robert was lightly sedated and was now alert enough for the session to begin.

"Robert I want you to listen to the sound of my voice, can you hear me?"

"Yes," he replied in a robotic manner.

"I want you to think back as far as you can remember, can you do that."

Robert's eyes twitched but remained closed.

"Ok, I want you to think back to being a little boy and let me know when you have reached your bedroom Robert; can you do that for me?"

"Yes."

Robert laid strapped at the chest, hands and feet to a metal gurney. He was placed in the observation room for this session. Robert became unpredictable as his moods swung. After reviewing the last of his sessions, the department chairs at Sox thought it best to induce hypnosis. They wanted to uncover exactly what lay in the recesses of Robert's mind. Three years had passed since his arrival at Sox and they were no further in their understanding of Robert's mind than they were the building of the pyramids. Robert remained motionless on the gurney as he was suspended somewhere in his consciousness. There were leads and monitors of differing nature attached to Robert so that his brain wave patterns and heart rate could be monitored. It wasn't often that hypnosis was used at Sox, more often than not medication was the preferred management choice with patients as disturb as Robert had shown himself to be.

Several sessions with Dr. Lieon revealed that Robert hated being with Ana, in fact he stated that he wished, she didn't exist at all. Though Ana sought to protect Robert when she could, he wanted to rid her from his life.

"Are you in your room now Robert?"

"No."

"Robert where are you?"

"I am standing in the hallway."

The monitors showed a constant brainwave pattern, his heart was steady and his pulse was calm.

"What are you doing in the hall Robert?"

"I'm looking through the door."

"Can you tell me what you see, what is happening that has you staring through the door?"

"I see legs. I see stockings the kind that look like a fisherman's net. I see a flowered dress. Oh no she is coming."

"What's happening Robert, who's coming?"

Robert's heartrate quicken and his eyes twitched.

"Tell me what is going on; where are you."

"You have to be quiet or she will hear you."

"Who will hear me Robert, who is coming?"

Robert's eye moved quickly under their lids as he spoke.

"It's ok Robert I am here; I won't let anything happen to you. Tell me what is going on, what do you see?

"No, no, I don't want to." Robert pleaded.

"Robert what is going on, what is happening to you?"

Robert began to move about on the gurney as though he was trying to free himself. The recording of his brain waves lit up like the Fourth of July. His pulse was now up to one hundred and forty beats per minutes.

"Robert, listen to the sound of my voice. Focus I will get you back to safety. Robert can you hear me?"

Dr. Allison began to count backwards trying to awaken Robert from the hypnosis. His heart rate gradually began to slow as she spoke low and methodically.

"When the bell rings you will be here at Sox, in the present, you will no longer be a little boy in your home, do you understand?"

Robert didn't reply.

Dr. Allison rung the bell and Robert opened his eyes.

"Robert its Dr. Allison do you know where you are?"

There was still no reply from Robert, his heart rate returned to normal, but his brain wave pattern appeared off, not as though he was still under hypnosis but different.

"Robert."

Dr. Allison called for Robert but he did not answer. She stood up from where she was seated and walked across the floor with a small pin light in her hand. Dr. Allison check Robert's pupils; she hoped that he had not suffered some sort of seizure while in the trance. His eyes were open and his pupils were normal.

"Robert can you hear me."

"I can hear you, but who is Robert?"

Dr. Allison was confused by the question.

"You are of course."

"I'm not Robert."

"Well who are you then?"

"I'm Diane."

~ 7 ~

There was a knock on the open door.

"Dr. Lieon, Dr. Lieon are you in here?"

Johnathan walked into Emalee's office carrying three separate DVD discs in his hand. He thought it odd that her door was wide open but proceeded to leave the discs on her bookshelf, unaware that she lied unconscious on the floor behind her desk. Johnathan placed the discs on Emalee's shelf and turn the light out in the corner before leaving. A groggy Dr. Lieon came to on the cold floor of her office. She adjusted her eyes to the darkness as her head began to throb, a painful reminder that she had been attacked. She felt around for the corner of her desk. She could barely see as her eyes tried to focus on the minimal light that shown through her office window. Emalee pushed against her chair as she crawled to restroom. The coldness of the bathroom floor sent a chill through her. Emalee braced herself against the door frame as she stood. She felt against the wall to find the light switch. She was stunned at the sight of the half-moon shape bruise that was beginning to form on her porcelain skin. Her dark brown hair had come undone from its bun and her eyes looked haggard. Emalee instantly thought of Edward.

He had become unhinged. She could faintly remember his words, as she turned to leave the restroom. Their conversation flashed through her mind. Edward mentioned something about remembering, but remembering what? Emalee stumbled through her office until she regained her balance. She opened the door to her office and saw a few interns down the hall. She wanted to cry out to them but felt too weak. As she made her way down the hall she came to Ana's room. Emalee thought of what to say to her about her recent absence but that would have to wait, she needed to get to the front desk. Emalee had no idea how much time had passed or how long she remained unconscious. She slowly walked passed Ana's room on the opposite side of the door, hoping that Ana would not see her. Just as she got beyond the door she heard Ana speaking to someone. Emalee was sure that Robert had been removed from the room. She heard Ana growing upset in the conversation. Emalee crossed the hall and pressed her ear against the door.

"I can't tell her, she won't believe me."

"You have no other choice." a male voice replied to Ana.

"I've tried to tell her about *The Others* and she won't listen. No one ever listens, until it's too late."

"It's up to you, you have to make her believe or it will be on your hands. Do you want that? Do you want her blood on your hands Ana?"

Emalee heard Ana sobbing through the door, she needed to get to the front desk, but she also needed to know who was in the room with Ana. More importantly, why there would be blood on her hands? Emalee felt around in her coat pocket for Ana's room key. The room was dark, just the light from the moon shining down on the old wooden chair that Ana often sat in. Ana sat on her bed with her bare feet hanging just above the floor, she was facing Robert's bed. Emalee flipped on the light.

"Ana who is in here with you?"

"Dr. Lieon! Ana exclaimed, "You're back."

Emalee saw tears in Ana's eyes despite the enthusiasm she exuded.

"Ana who were you talking to?

Emalee looked at Robert's bed but there was no one there. The covers were neatly tucked and the pillows had not been disturbed.

"Where have you been Dr. Lieon, it's been days. Seems like weeks." Ana spoke rapidly as she approached Emalee.

"Here, you can sit here Dr. Lieon," Ana said as she pointed to her favorite chair.

"I am so glad to see you, what have you been up to?"

Ana reminded Emalee of a little child, as her eyes and thoughts ran all over. Emalee reached up to her head wincing as she touched the fresh bruise.

"Oh Dr. Lieon what happen? Did you fall, did something hit you, or did you walk into a wall? I use to walk into walls all the time when I was little."

Emalee watched as Ana rambled on.

"Ana I am going to ask you again who where you speaking to a moment ago?

Ana's eyes lowered as she took her place on the end of the bed. She placed her legs on the bed covering them with a blanket.

"There is no one in here but me Dr. Lieon."

Ana avoided making eye contact with Emalee; she knew Dr. Lieon didn't believe her.

"Ana, I know that you are in here, but who else was with you?"

Ana didn't respond, she merely shook her head.

"I know someone was in here, I could hear them, I heard you say..."

Emalee stopped; she realized that no one could be in the room. She'd used the key to open the door;

there was no other way in or out. There were no other doors, just the window. Ana was far worst that what she initially thought. Ana was showing clear signs of a personality disorder. She had begun to manifest an alternate reality, probably in an attempt to deal with all the abuse she suffered as a young child or as a direct result of Robert's rage. Ana mentioned *The Others* before, had she been trying to tell her that she was aware that she was jumping from one personality to another. Emalee's mind raced as she wondered how she could have been so blind. She'd let her research consume her to the point that she wasn't even aware that her own patient was suffering from an additional mental disorder.

"Ana, Ana." Dr. Lieon called out.

Ana looked up at Dr. Lieon and smiled.

"I'm listening Ana, is there something you want to talk about, *The Others* maybe."

Ana looked around the room as though she was checking to see if the coast was clear before speaking.

"I tried to tell you Dr. Lieon."

"Tried to tell me what Ana?"

"I tried to tell you about *The Others*, but you wouldn't listen."

"I am listening now, what do they want? I mean, do they want something from you?"

Ana sat with her hand in her lap, she slowly rolled her thumbs one over the other.

"Ana do they want something from you?"

"Sometimes they just appear. They don't say anything, they just watch."

"And the other times?"

Emalee was anxious to know what *The Others* wanted to from Ana. She was surprised that she was so aware of them. Most patients that suffered from a personality disorder did not possess the knowledge of the other identities. They often acted independently of each other, making sure to protect their own individualities. Ana was a unique case. She was quite aware that *The Others* existed; she was even cognitive of their interactions with her own being.

"Ana what do they want with you the other times?"

Before Ana could reply, the door to the room opened.

"There you are Dr. Lieon; I have been looking all over for you. Come with me, I need to speak with you about Robert."

Ana dropped her head as Dr. Allison led Dr. Lieon out of the room. She could see Dr. Allison smirked as she closed the door behind them. Ana wanted to tell Dr. Lieon everything, but she wondered if *The Others* would let her. Would they let her tell Dr. Lieon the truth? Ana crawled to the top of her bed and waited, soon it would be time for medicine. Maybe tonight she could sleep peacefully. She wondered where Robert was as the pain in her arm begun to awaken. Though she hated to admit it, Robert was better at keeping *The Others* away than she was. They seemed to be afraid of him, for that matter so was she.

~ 8 ~

J ohnathan stood at the front desk ogling the lanky redhead. She pretended to chart files as he stood there rambling about his plans for the future. His words came out behind crooked teeth and were accompanied by a warm smile. Johnathan thought she wore red well; it showed like a sunset against her pale complexion. Redheads were known to be fair, but she was the palest he'd ever seen by far, even Dr. Allison seemed olive skin in comparison.

"So what do you think about Dr. Emalee?"

She glanced at Johnathan but didn't reply.

"I mean she is easier to work with than Dr. Allison don't you think?"

Johnathan saw his efforts to make small talk were going nowhere; he looked out the glass front windows and could see a few figures walking across the courtyard. The broken post lamps, made it hard for him to make out who any of the figures were. The redhead stared straight ahead at her charts as though Johnathan didn't exist.

"So where are you from?"

The receptionist exhaled deeply as he continued his inquisition. She reviewed the last of her charts before speaking.

"Let me make this clear, I'm not interested, get it."

Johnathan was hurt that she didn't have the decency to even make eye contact. He only wanted a little friendly conversation to cut through the remaining hours left on his shift.

"Yea I get it, have a good night," he replied coldly as he turned from the window.

Johnathan wondered why she'd been so rude. The receptionist hadn't worked at Sox long come to think of it. He witnessed her speaking with a few of the orderlies, but she mostly kept to herself. It was no wonder Dr. Emalee wasn't impressed with her. She displayed the personality of a rabid dog. Johnathan walked back to the AV room feeling rejected. He thought to himself, there was nothing wrong with being friendly. The more he thought about how rude the receptionist was the angrier he became.

He disliked rude people, and considering they were working with mental health patients, rudeness had no place here. What right did she have to ignore people? Johnathan paced back and forth in the AV room when something in the assessment room caught is attention.

The room was dark except for a small object that reflected the light. Whatever it was twinkled like a little star on the floor near the wall of art. Johnathan lifted the lights in the room for a better view, but the object vanished. His curiosity got the better of him and he wanted to check it out. The last thing he needed was for something to be in one of the rooms and one of the doctors became injured because of it. You never knew what to expect from the patients at Sox. Some were harmless like little butterflies and others where completely deranged. Jonathan cut the light out to the room and left the object to shine.

There was no one in the control room to buzz him in and out of the self-locking door of the assessment room, so he grabbed a chair to prop the door open. The small object twinkled in the corner of the room near the zig-zag painting. The room was dark except for the lighting in the AV room. Johnathan reversed the glass to the room so he could see in and anyone else could see out. As he bent down to pick up the small object, Johnathan paused as he thought he saw someone out the corner of his eye. He looked around quickly, but no one was there. Johnathan grabbed at the small object, but it was entangled in the carpet fibers. He lowered himself to his hands and knees as he tugged on what appeared to be a ring of some sort. Just what he needed; a stupid ring that a patient could swallow or use to hurt someone. Johnathan felt the hairs on the back of his neck rise; he snapped around in the dark room but again nothing. He thought to himself, this place was really doing a number on him. He began working at Sox only a year ago and a year already felt like a lifetime. Finally he freed the small shiny object from the carpet. It wasn't a ring at all; he wasn't sure what it was. Johnathan sat back on his feet as he held the small metal object up to the light from the AV room. He rotated it between his fingers so that he could get a better look.

The object fell from Johnathan's hand as he grasped for his neck. Johnathan fell back onto his buttocks as some strange force grabbed him around his neck. His feet kicked and his legs shook as he clawed at the fabric as it crushed his airway. Johnathan blinked quickly trying to take in as much information as he could as he fought for his life. With one hand extended over his head, he could feel the bulge of muscles in the arm of the person who was unmistakably trying to end his life. Johnathan tried to twist onto his side in an attempt to take his attacker by surprise or hoping he could at least knock them off balance. His every move was met with one just as powerful. Johnathan began to feel lightheaded from the lack of oxygen that he was being deprived of. He could no longer feel his legs as they grew heavy and immobile. With both hands now gripped around the fabric encircling his neck, Johnathan thought he smelt the scent of Dr. Allison's perfume before he closed his eyes. Johnathan fought with all his might to stay awake, to stay alive but it was to no avail. The fabric tightened pressing the edges of his fingers against his neck until his chest no longer rose and fell. Johnathan's body was thrown to the floor as the dark figure moved about the room. The figure bent down and placed the small metal object near Johnathan's feet. The figure stood there for a moment admiring their work. Johnathan's pale face lied facing the light of the AV and a blue flowered scarf was placed in his hand before the door to the assessment room was closed.

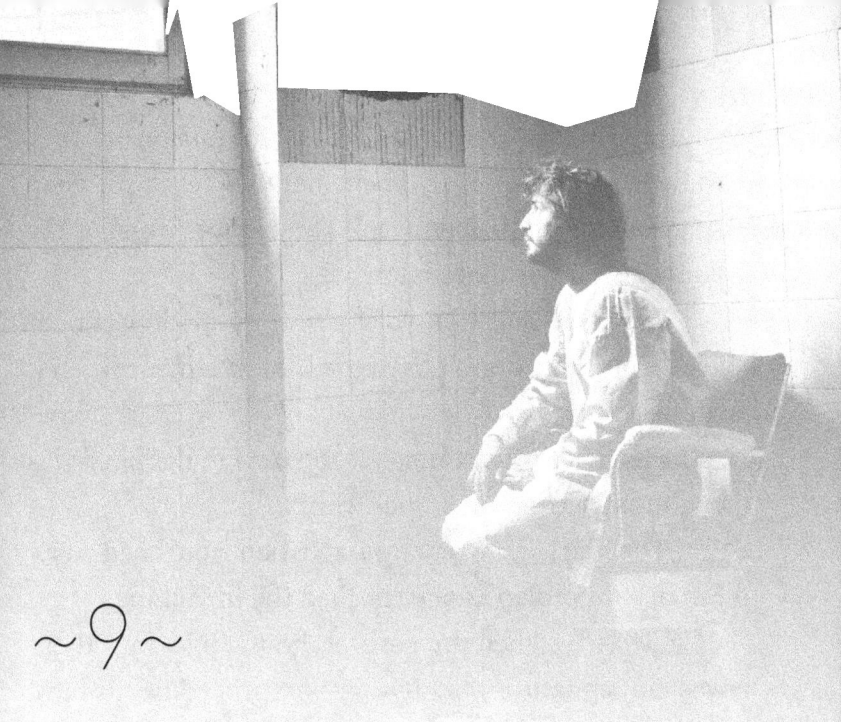

~9~

malee stood in the halls of Sox with Dr. Allison wondering what all the commotion was about. Why was Allison tracking her down? It was late and unlike her to be at Sox after dark.

"I've been looking all over for you."

Emalee looked at Allison with bewilderment.

"My goodness; are you alright what happen to your head?"

Allison asked as she tried brush away the dark strands of hair that were now glued to Emalee's face with dried blood. Momentarily she'd forgotten about her encounter with Edward. Emalee touched her fresh wound and winced.

"I will tell you about it later. I need to check to see how long ago a patient left."

Emalee explained the details to Allison as they walked the halls. Dr. Allison berated her with each step for not immediately call security or pressing the panic button for that matter.

"Emalee I question your ability to be department lead. You clearly don't have the best judgment when it comes to patients."

Allison's words stung, but the pain in her head was beginning to drown out her words.

"That girl is never around when you need her." Emalee mumbled as she checked the in/out log.

Edward signed in several hours ago but there was no signature out. It was Sox procedure to have a doctor sign a patient in and out, but since she was left on the floor unconscious there would have been no one available. Emalee thought for a second that maybe Edward was still somewhere inside of Sox, but that wouldn't make any sense. He wouldn't have stuck around after knocking her out, would he? She wondered if the redhead had just let him leave without questioning, she wasn't the most observant.

"Have you seen, oh, what is her name?" Emalee asked frustrated.

"No why?"

Emalee felt bad enough, she didn't want to have to explain that she wasn't sure if her attacker was running loose inside Sox. Emalee turned around and closed her eyes as she leaned her back against the desk.

Why don't we just call security and have them look at the tapes. By now they would have seen if anything was out of the ordinary Emalee thought to herself.

"I didn't know she had children."

"Who?"

'The receptionist."

"Why do you think she has children?'

"Why else would she have a toy at her desk?"

Emalee turned around to see what Dr. Allison was babbling on about. Her eyes grew large which shot searing pain through her wound.

"Where did you get that?" Emalee yelled.

"It was right here on the floor, what is wrong with you?"

Emalee could not believe her eyes. In Dr. Allison's hand was the toy fire engine her father had given her. She must be mistaken, she was sure she'd placed the engine in her desk before her meeting with Edward.

"Give it to me!" She demanded.

Emalee held out her hand as a stunned and confused Dr. Allison handed over the toy. She flipped the toy over and as she expected her initials were etched on the bottom of the engine.

"Emalee what is going on?"

Emalee's temple throbbed as she could feel her pressure rising. The room swayed as she grew more heated. It was bad enough that she was a poor receptionist if you could even call her that, but she was a thief as well.

"You don't look so hot." Dr. Allison said as she stood there gazing at Emalee.

"Hey, what's going on up here?" The overly perky receptionist approached her desk unaware that the toy engine had been discovered.

"You tell me? Emalee retorted snidely as she pointed to the engine.

"That old thing?"

She said dismissively as she took to her seat.

"Johnathan left it up here. I was just going to throw it out."

"Where is Johnathan? Dr. Allison asked.

"He was up here about an hour ago; I haven't seen him since I told him I wasn't interested in him."

Emalee grew so heated from the sound of her voice that she lunged across the desk dropping the toy engine.

"Emalee!" Dr. Allison exclaimed.

Emalee's eyes were dilated, her face was flushed, and she looked possessed as she clawed at the redhead. Dr. Allison immediately called for security as she pleaded with Emalee to calm down. Emalee rounded the corner of her desk with hate in her eyes causing the redhead to retreat into the corner.

"Aren't you going to do anything? She asked Dr. Allison as she stood there in disbelief.

Dr. Allison reached in her pocket hoping she had remembered the syringe. She only used Midazolam a few times since she arrived at Sox and now was one of those times. Just as Emalee grabbed for the receptionist, Dr. Allison emptied the syringe into her right arm. Emalee turned her attention to Dr. Allison who moved away allowing security to intervene.

"Why?" Was all Emalee could mutter as the effects of the drugs took hold.

"Take her to the observation room," Dr. Allison instructed as two broad shoulder men carried Emalee's limp body away.

"She is just as crazy as everyone else here."

The pale faced receptionist said as she and Dr. Allison watched Emalee disappear.

"Is she?

The receptionist shocked by the reply quickly looked at the floor. "I suggest you get this cleaned up and while you're at it locate Edward White. The log said he never check out."

"Who?"

An annoyed Dr. Allison walked over to the patient log and pointed.

"Mr. White."

The redhead glanced at the login.

"There was no Mr. White here today and I have been here all afternoon."

"He must have arrived while you were away from your desk, Emalee signed him in."

"I told you she was crazy, she signs someone in every day. I never see who it is, and I never see them leave."

"What are you talking about?"

"See for yourself."

The redhead receptionist pulled out a stack of log sheets, all showing different patient names about the same time every day and exactly two hours later the patients were logged out.

"Where are you when this happens?"

"Most of the time I am here when she comes to check the book. I see her scribble something and leave. I am here when she comes back. Both times no one is with her."

"Just have security review footage around these times for the pass week."

"Suit yourself, but they won't find anything."

Dr. Allison took a copy of one of the log sheets. She wanted to speak to Emalee once she came to in the observation room. Hopefully by then she would have regained her senses. She understood that she was under a great strain but this wasn't making any sense. Dr. Allison examined the log sheet as she walked the halls of Sox when she noticed the times on the log. Emalee was adamant about her schedule and the times that she saw her patients. After thinking for a moment she realized that the entries all corresponded with the times of her group sessions. Maybe she was trying to introduce a patient into group. She'd mentioned before testing her research; this had to be what was going on, or was it?

~10~

malee laid on the cold metal gurney. She shivered as her body adjusted to the temperature of the room. The pain in her arm woke her. She could barely remember anything other than Dr. Allison stabbing her in the harm. She slide off the gurney and tried the knob on the door but it was locked as she expected. She banged hard on the door, hoping that someone was nearby. She was all too familiar with this room. She'd spent countless hours observing patients and taking notes on their every action. Emalee walked back to the middle of the room where she stood waving her arms back and forth over her head. If Johnathan was watching, by now he could clearly see that she was lucid, but there was no one there. Dr. Allison was off trying to make sense of the logs as Emalee paced around the room. What happened, her head was still hurting from being slammed against her desk. Emalee sat back on the gurney, she remembered speaking to Ana but after that things were a blur. As she sat, she could hear that someone was fiddling with keys. She anxiously sat there hoping that Dr. Allison had come to let her out. The door opened quickly.

"What are you doing in here and how did you get in here?"

"Shh, I came to help you."

Emalee was both shocked and confused to find Ana standing in the room.

"How did you get out of your room?

"That is not important; we don't have much time to get you out of here."

"Ana, you are not making sense."

Emalee believed that Ana was now experiencing a full on psychotic break. Her first instinct was to coax her back to reality, but she thought it far better to play along. The longer she could keep her talking the better it was. She needed her to stay as calm as possible until she could get her to her room.

"Ok Ana, why do we need to leave?"

Ana moved over to Emalee as she looked around and whispered.

"*The Others* are coming."

"About that Ana, how many others are they."

Ana looked up at Dr. Emalee as though she was confused by her question.

"We don't have time Dr. Emalee we have to go now."

As Emalee stepped down from the gurney, she wondered how Ana knew where she was, and how she'd gotten the keys to the room.

"Ana, stop, wait," she said pulling away. Ana grabbed her wrist.

"Please don't be mad with me Dr. Emalee, I just want to help."

"I know you do Ana, and I appreciate it," she said softly. "But how did you get out of your room and where did you get those keys?"

Emalee eyes focused on the small metal skull ring that hung from the keys. She knew those keys, where had she seen them before...Johnathan. Emalee remained calm; she didn't need to spook Ana at a time like this.

"The redhead let me out; she lets me out every day. She told me where I could find you and to hurry before *The Others* came."

Ana opened the door slowly as Emalee tried to process what she said, Ana gasped.

"I thought I would find you here."

Ana and Emalee slowly backed up. Pings of tension mounted in Emalee's stomach.

"Were you two planning on going somewhere?"

Ana's shoulders curved as she hurried to hide behind Emalee.

"Robert!"

"Were you expecting someone else?" He asked coldly as he closed the door.

Emalee surveyed the room but she knew she wouldn't find anything that she could use for protection. She could feel Ana clawing at the back of her lab coat. Emalee grabbed one end of the gurney and pulled it close creating a small barrier between Robert and the both of them.

Robert loomed over them, never had she been so afraid. How did he know that they would be in observation room? Now was not the time for Q & A. Robert had proven to be the more adept of the two, he was quicker to catch on to the mind games and better skilled at avoidance than Ana. Emalee could only hope to somehow maneuver herself closer to the door so she and Ana could get free. By now someone should have noticed that both Ana and Robert were missing. Emalee reached in her pocket but her syringe was not there. It must have fallen out when they brought her into the room. Robert stood in front of the door blocking the only exit to the room.

"Come here Ana" he demanded.

"Ana don't you move."

Emalee could hear Ana whimpering behind her.

"You leave her alone!" Emalee yelled.

"And who is going to protect you Emalee?" Robert said with a smirk.

"Any moment someone will be in the other room watching you, us and they will come in."

"Don't you get it, no one is looking for you?"

"Of course they are, I have patients and when I don't make my rounds they will be concerned. Beside they know I am in here."

Robert laughed heartily as Emalee tried to explain why she was so important.

"The room is monitored Robert even you had to know that."

"So it is. Ana" he again called for her.

Ana peered from behind Dr. Emalee, and looked into Roberts cold eyes. Ana remember the way he would look at her when they were children. She hated the way he made her feel.

"Ana you know what to do."

"Robert no," Ana pleaded.

"Ana what is he talking about?"

"I tried to tell you, I tried to warn you about *The Others*."

"Ana for God's sake what are you talking about?"

Emalee could feel Ana's chest rising and falling against her back.

"Calm down and talk slowly."

"Tell the precious doctor what you did Ana."

"I didn't do anything, it was *The Others*."

"Ok Ana, what did *The Others* do?"

The room was quiet, neither Robert nor Ana spoke for several minutes.

"They did bad things Dr. Emalee."

"Ana whatever they did, I will not blame you. I only want to help you."

"You can't even help yourself." Robert retorted as he moved closer.

"Ana tell me!" Emalee demanded turning to face Ana.

"They killed Johnathan."

Emalee placed her hand over her mouth.

"And they killed Dr. Allison."

Emalee immediately felt sick as the words slowly flowed from Ana's mouth.

"Why Ana, why?'

Tears welled in Ana's eyes as Dr. Emalee looked at her in disbelief.

"I knew you would blame me. I told you about *The Others* but you blame me, but it wasn't me."

"I believe you Ana."

"No you don't, you never believe me. I told you *The Others* were coming, I told you!"

Ana was almost yelling.

"Come here Ana." Again Robert demanded for Ana to move.

"Don't worry Ana I won't let him hurt you anymore.

Robert moved so close to Dr. Emalee and Ana that he stood just on the other side of the gurney. He leaned forward and mouthed the words *run*.

~11~

The pressure, Emalee knew this feeling all too well. She could feel the grip tighten around her throat. She could hear voices but she was unable to distinguish what was being said. She fought as hard as she could. There were screams mixed with laughter as she faded in and out of consciousness.

"Remember, you have to remember."

She thought she heard the voice of a small child. As Emalee fought to free herself, an image caught her attention as the blue flowered scarf continued to cut off her air. There in the corner of the room holding her fire engine stood a little boy about six years old. There he stood with a single tear rolling down his cheek as he watched her fight. Where had he come from, how did he get in here? Emalee closed her eyes as she prepared to take her last breath. She reopened them to see Ana on one side and Robert on the other. It was like there was some strange tug of war and she was caught in the middle.

Emalee turned her head and tried desperately to catch a few fleeting breaths as the door to the observation room opened. A tall shadow came closer as Ana and Robert backed away. She could see the little boy coil in fear as the shadow got closer.

"No, no please he pleaded.

Emalee wanted to do something to help him, but what, she couldn't even help herself. Emalee quickly un-wrapped the scarf from around her neck as she sat up. Both Ana and Robert were gone.

"Leave him alone!" She shouted but the shadow didn't respond.

Emalee felt faint as she stood to her feet. She looked at the little boy who all but buried his head in his arms as the figure tore at his clothes. Emalee looked at the open door. She was faced with a tough decision. Go for help or save the child. Surely she could get security but what would be of the boy?

Emalee's chest heaved as she all but hyperventilated deciding if she should save herself or the child. She backed up against the gurney as the figure began to consume the small boy. She lunged with all her might as the figure turned around and knocked her against the wall. Emalee hit the back of her head as she slid down the wall. Emalee saw the boy crawling to her as the figure approached. Emalee grabbed for the child and held him in her arms as she closed her eyes and prepared for what would come.

"You've been a bad boy Robert."

Emalee opened her eyes; she couldn't believe what she saw. She wasn't in the observation room at Sox but her bedroom. She stood in corner of her childhood bedroom. There stood the little boy from Sox. What was going on?

"How many times must I tell you to call me mother?" The voice yelled.

"But but..." Emalee could hear the boy's voice tremble as he spoke.

"Get up and put this dress on."

The boy was yanked by his right arm as he stood barefoot in his underwear. His dark brown locks were pulled back as tears ran down his face.

"Stop all that crying."

A red and white stripped dress was forced down over his body.

"Oh don't you look pretty." The voice said as it mocked him.

"Turn around and let me see.

The small boy stood in the red and white dress with his hair in a ponytail like a doll on display.

"I have to go to the bathroom he whined."

The boy was hurried down the halls across the cold wooden floors.

"Leave the door open so I can watch."

He lifted the hem of the red and white dress and pulled down his underwear. He stood in front of the toilet with his feet slightly apart as he relieved himself. He hadn't been allowed to use the restroom all morning and his stomach had begun to hurt. A hot slap across his face caught him off guard as he emptied his bladder.

"I told you little girls sit." He touched his stinging cheek as he stood there with his underwear around his ankles.

"I see I am going to have to teach you a lesson."

A handful of his hair was grabbed as he was drug down the hall, leaving his underwear behind.

"No, please no, I will be good, he cried out."

Emalee stood frozen against the wall as his little body was flung across the bed. The room was pink with white. There were porcelain dolls that sat high on the shelves. All of the clothes were neatly folded, even those in the hamper. A flowered tea set sat quaintly next to a charcoal drawing on the little table beside the bed.

"No daughter of mine will stand, you will act properly like a lady."

"No mommy please."

His body was pinned to the bed as his legs were forced open.

"Well what do we have here?"

When he became frighten things just seemed to happen on their own accord. He was gripped hard. Emalee couldn't believe her eyes.

"I know what we will do, I just cut it off, and then you will be a proper lady. Would you like that?

"No mommy, I'm Robert. I am a boy." He pleaded.

Emalee watched as mother pulled and yanked at the little boy's private, threating to remove it all. She watched as his brown locks were grabbed and forced against the red hairs and pale skin. The more Robert resisted the more he was forced to take the long barrel down his small throat.

Emalee slid to the floor as memories began to flood. Her early memories of her father were happy and playful, but were they real? She was four when mother died, not yet old enough to go to school. She remembered how sad her father was. Father said they were supposed to be together forever. The day of the funeral it was just the two of them. Mother wore a pale blue dress with a blue flowered scarf around her neck. Father always said how much she looked like mother. The next morning she awoke to father wearing one of mother's dresses. At first it seemed odd but then it was like make believe. He would say all the things she would say and he would give hugs and kisses just like mother. Months passed and father still hadn't returned to work. They idea of them being apart was too much for him to bear. They would play dressed up and then one day he placed a small box on the table. In the box lied a pink dress and a winter wheat colored wig. It was all a lie, Robert, Ana all of the others. What was going on? Emalee became confused. What did she have to do with Robert and Ana? This wasn't her life, her story. She had a happy childhood; though there were only a few memories they were all happy.

Emalee could still hear her mother saying

"If you see something bad, close your eyes and tell yourself it's not real three times and when you open them again, it will be gone."

She repeated the saying over and over for the next three years. Everyday father would come into her room dress like his mother. At first it wasn't so bad but then he began to make Emalee wear dresses and the wig daily. Being Robert was the earliest memory Emalee possessed. It was so bad at first but soon father stopped calling her Robert and began to call her Ana. As Robert she would protest and would be beaten and choked; seeing Robert gasp for air excited Father. One time Robert's arm was broken because he'd forgotten to line his dolls up neatly. Father said that he looked so much like mother that he should have been a girl. Robert would stare at the black and white paintings that hung on the wall and would imagine himself lost inside as he endured the daily torture. He learned not to have feelings; feelings only lead to more pain. One night after father made Robert, who was dressed as *Ana,* do the things mother would have done, Robert went down stairs to the study to find father. A tired and weary Robert came down the stairs and quietly slipped into the kitchen. Robert searched through all the drawers for something heavy. He didn't want to play pretend anymore; he didn't want to be Ana anymore. He could hear father moving in the room when he saw his fire engine on the floor. Robert quietly tiptoed across the dusty floor in his pink dress and picked up the engine before smashing it against father's head. Robert hit the engine against Edward Morrison's head until his little arms fell limp. The next morning Robert packed his fire engine and few items in his small pack back and left the little gray house on Sox Ave.

Years went by and Robert was able to survive the world unnoticed. He had fallen in love, but his love was rejected. It wasn't until he heard Ana's voice as he wrapped his mother's scarf around his love's neck that he knew she never really left him. One day after a public fight with Ana, they were taken to Mazella to be treated. Dr. White was kind and understood Robert. Robert didn't understand why he no longer wanted to help him. Dr. White was just like all the others, they would appear for a while and then leave him when he needed them the most. After Dr. White's departure, Dr. Emalee began to treat them both. Dr. Emalee was fond of Ana, it didn't matter that Robert was the one in need of help. If he was going to ever survive he need to be free of Ana and something had to be done about Dr. Emalee.

~12~

There was nothing more stressful than dealing with new patients and Dr. White was no exception to this. He had recently been hired as the Chair of the prestigious Mazzella Institute of Psychiatry upon high referral from Sox Psychiatric Facility. This was a great place to practice due to the wide variety of psychiatry illness they saw on a daily basis. As Dr. White stared out his office window, he began to think back over the past few months. Life was relatively quiet and quiet was the thing he needed most. With the death of his colleague, Dr. White fought to regain his daily regimen. Lately his thoughts were consumed with all that he'd left behind. He knew that his obsession with the past was unhealthy but from time to time his mind seemed to wander. Dr. White couldn't remember the last time he saw the outside world, as he was lost in taking on his new role as the Department Chair. He sat in his office moving the small metal fire truck back and forth across his desk. It was a present from Dr. Emalee, their last exchange was all but endearing. In the all the time that he had spent working with her, not once had she lost her composure. That was until he announced his departure.

Her words rung in his ears as he thought back on their final exchange. Emmalee had become much more than a colleague, she was his confident and for that matter his only friend. Dr. White lived a solitary life for most of his existence. It wasn't until he reached the facility that he was able to spread his wings and become a more dominate force. Dr. White watched as the fire engine rolled to the edge of the desk appearing to hover. He contemplated where he should catch the toy or whether to allow it to fall to the ground. He took his fingers and gently pulled on the rear bumper allowing it to roll back onto the dark brown desk. Dr. White was found of the woodwork and carvings that adorned the desk. There were flecks of auburn strands entangled around the rear wheel of the small engine that caught his attention. He slowly pulled at the strands; he held the fibers up to the light in his office as he examined them closely. He rolled the strands between his fingers and wondered where they came from. He placed them to his nose inhaling their intoxicating perfume. He immediately thought of Emalee as the smell of jasmine and vanilla overtook him. Dr. White laid a few of the strands on a napkin and thought to himself that he should keep them safe. He wouldn't allow himself to be overtaken by his emotions; there was no time for that, as there were meetings to attend. Dr. White looked at his black leather planner where his initials were embossed in gold, and saw that he was to see a new patient. There was a red file on the corner of his desk. As he flipped through the file, he noted several things about the patient. It was rare in his position as chair that he would see patients. In fact he was assured that this would be more of an administrative role. While he loved analyzing the trappings of a patient's mind, it became more taxing over the years. He noted in the patient's file that she suffered from paranoia, depression, schizophrenia, delusions, and bi-polar disorder. Never before in his career had Dr. White experienced a patient with this level of psychosis. He wondered why the patient was assigned to him at all. Maybe this was all some sort of mistake. He thought for a moment that maybe it was more of a consult for him to recommend a course of treatment perhaps. As he moved through the file Dr. White spotted a note in the back flap of the folder.

"Patient request Dr. White."

This was peculiar he thought to himself. How would a patient even know to ask for him? In fact, his last year he purposely avoided treating anyone. As he closed the file he became more agitated with the whole idea. His agitation grew as he glimpsed a stain on the wrist of his freshly starched shirt. He immediately arose from his desk walking over to the small closet in his office. Neatly tucked away were twelve more blue pinstriped shirts. Heavily starched and all facing to the right. As he tore the stained shirt from his body, he fought the urge that was swelling inside of him. How could he have been so careless? Dr. White often did his sketches with a charcoal pencil. He came across the pen thinking a splash of color would be a nice change of pace. He meticulously buttoned each button and smoothed out the shirt as he adjusted his collar. He removed the leaking pen from his desk along with his torn dress shirt and neatly placed them in the wastebasket.

He checked his watch; there was still an hour before he was to meet the mystery patient. He took a sip of water from the red cup which sat on the window sill. He preferred his water at room temperature, as cold water often brought on severe headaches. He took a minute to gather himself. As he sat in the oversize chair near the window he observed the clouds playing hide and seek with sun. The thought amused him somehow. It was on a day like today when he met his first patient. Ana was a young woman in her late twenties. She was tall, thin, and plain. There was nothing striking about her. Her appearance was as bland as the office itself with its beige walls and dust brown furnishings. He began his session with his normal line of questioning. The patient fidgeted in her chair as she replied guardedly to his questions. Ana revealed that she had been depressed for some time. She spoke with a forced effort and reluctance that made Dr. White question her authenticity. The patient briefly described her childhood as though it was something as insignificant as buying bread from the store. Though her features were unremarkable at best he did take note of a long scar on the side of her neck. She showed undeniable signs of depression, but that didn't strike Dr. White as odd. The longer he observed her the more he thought the patient suffered from other mental disorders.

She spoke calmly and then become extremely agitated often speaking of herself in third person. He sat observing as she responded with annoyance at his calmness. It was important for him to remain aware of his reactions in order to assess the patient. He listened to her speak with an annoying monotone voice for hours on end. It became apparent that she was suffering from dissociative episodes and from time to time her consciousness would split. He suspected this from the onset of her treatment but her continual headaches and references to *The Others*, with no defined answers as to whom those others were, was a defining factor. Dr. White saw the patient only a couple more times before she began to refuse to see him. She stated that she felt Dr. White was plotting against her. She told him over and over of some mystery man who wanted her dead. The patient was adamant that he had been trying to kill her since she was a child. He felt that she made great progress in learning that her episodes began sometime in her early childhood after her parents died. She somehow managed to survive in her own delusions throughout the early part of her adult life. There was no mention of a romantic interest of any kind or the want for one. Her non-existent social life was due in part to the amount of time she became lost in her own delusions. On the last night Dr. White treated Ana, she was completely out of sorts. Her personalities were autonomous by this point.

At exactly 6:30 p.m. every day, Dr. White would stop by Ana's room to check on her. She faithfully sat in a small wooden chair by the window. He often wondered what she thought about as she looked out onto the courtyard. Rain or shine she would sit with bare feet in her thin gown and stare out the small window. He himself was a misfit and he sympathized with the patient. A world of isolation was tough on anyone, but especially those who thoughts often betrayed them. On this particular afternoon as he arrived to check on Ana he heard various voices exuding from the room as he approached. He hoped that she made a breakthrough by allowing herself to interact with the others in the facility. But his hopes were quickly dashed when he saw Ana in a full blown episode. Dr. White stood in awe as the patient went on in a similar fashion as someone possessed. Her normally high pitched voice morphed into a low growl as she took on a male persona. Her rounded shoulders squared off as the conversation continued. She sat unaware that she was being observed. How long she had been in this state? He observed with a kid like fascination as she easily switched personas. He watched as she rose from the chair and swiftly moved across the floor stopping just short of the bed. Dr. White looked on as she focused her attention on the wall behind the bed. She shook her head as if she was objecting as she flung herself into the wall. Dr. White fought the urge he had to run over to check on her, unsure if his touch would send her deeper into her psychosis. He inched closer as she grabbed at her arm. He could see tears as they welled up in her eyes, then she hung her head.

"You didn't have to push me; that hurt."

She never looked up, her gaze still focused downward as she spoke. Dr. White searched for the words, but they became lost in his throat as he stepped backwards causing the floor to creek.

"You should go now before *The Others* arrive." She said in a soft voice.

"Ana are you sure?"

She nodded but her eyes remained closed, her body eerily still despite her apparent pain.

"I will be back," he whispered.

"Hello, Dr. White," she said with as much exuberance as a small child.

He was amazed at how quickly her tone shifted. He paused before turning the key, wondering if the patient was about to display yet another personality.

"When you see Dr. Emalee, would you tell her I miss her, she has not been by in some time."

Dr. White smiled and nodded at the patient's request before closing the door. He looked back in on her one last time before departing to his office. There she sat on the cold wooden floor in a pleasant conversation with herself.

~13~

// Begin Note: *Today is April 1, 2016. The patient was found walking the halls, seemingly to respond to unidentified stimuli. The patient was dressed in the standard hospital issued clothing. Upon further inspection it is still not understood how patient was able to exit room without force. Patient was well-mannered until asked to return to their room. Patient exhibited great fear and resistance at the idea of returning to housing quarters. After additional time was given patient relented. An alternative location was suggested and patient agreed. With an escort of myself and two orderlies, the patient was ushered into the observation room. Patient has displayed the trait of multiple personalities, mixed with delusions. Patient has been seen displaying the personality of a female named Ana as associated with childhood trauma. Patient struggles with given name of Robert and often displays violent tendencies when Robert is present. Thought the more domineering of the two personalities, Ana shows signs of the Alpha personality. Equally interesting as seen in observation is the patient's ability to create various roles of medical professionals by the name of Dr. Lieon, Dr. Allison and Dr. White. Patient has also displayed the persona of a darker unknown male as well as the newest identity Edward White, with whom the patient struggles with. It is assumed that the patient has projected these personalities as a coping mechanism to deal with the many unknown identities that still reside within. In previous sessions patient disclosed the growing urge to hurt others in a similar manner to the abuse displayed in early childhood. It is my hope with additional treatment and medication, patient can be stabilized."*

~14~

I t was abnormal for the Robert to remain quiet. It was clear that he would lead this time around. His posture was ridged and he sat with his fist clenched. The muscles in his back were tight under the thin gown. It was always more challenging to deal with Robert than any of the others; you never knew exactly what he was thinking. The room held a distinct musk odor that seemed to agitate him as he continuously sniffed at the air.

"Robert are you up for a chat today?"

He cut his eyes but did not respond.

"Robert, you are the one that is here correct?"

"What's this all about?" Dr. White asked. His tone and diction were distinct in comparison to Robert's labored speech. He sat up in the chair with his back aligned perfectly in a matter of fact manner.

"He doesn't wish to speak to you, any of you." Dr. White continued.

"Well I wish to speak to him, I haven't heard from him in a while. Robert are you in there?"

Dr. White seemed genuinely surprised. "Really?" he said. "I hear from him all the time."

There were rumblings as if there was confusion about what to do or say next. The voices switched interchangeably and effortlessly as his body morphed from, stiff, to rounded shoulders.

"Ana?'

"No, Ana is sleeping, she needs her rest. It was a long night you know."

"Dr. Lieon?"

"Please call me Emalee, no need to be so formal."

"Emalee then; where is Robert I would like to speak with him."

Leaning back in the chair he crossed his legs at the knees as he pulled the gown down taking care to straighten the creases that formed.

"Don't worry Robert is safe. Dr. White is taking good care of him."

He smiled but it was more of a smirk.

"Since you are here, how have things been going with you?

"Things couldn't be better. Any day now I should here back if they will elect me as the Chair of the Department."

"You would like that wouldn't you?"

"Of course I would, who wouldn't. I have worked my ass off with these patients the last three years. I have created some ground breaking research to benefit those the rest of you have just cast away." He continued on but paused as if he heard a noise. His eyebrows drew closer as his legged dropped.

"Emalee?"

He shook his head from side to side; there was something unfamiliar about the energy he alluded.

"Who is present?"

There was no response. Years of training and researched showed that the best method of enacting a response from a patient is sometimes the most direct method.

"Can you tell me about Edward Morrison, did you know him?"

The words hung low and heavy in the room, but they were effective. The unidentified persona, winced at the mention of the name.

"Did you know of the horrible things he did to Robert?"

Suddenly his back stiffened.

"He didn't do those things to Robert, he did them to me!"

"Ana?"

"That's not my name he shouted."

"You are?

"I am Diane."

"Oh yes, my apologies, is that the name your Father gave you?"

"My father, you know nothing of my father!"

"Is Edward not your father?"

Rather than answer, he laughed lightly. Diane's existence was unknown like so many of the others.

"He was my lover, well that was until that little bitch came around."

His mouth drew up as though he had a vile taste in his mouth.

"Tell me about that."

"What is there to tell? Edward loved me, no he absolutely adored me. I was his everything." He paused as though he was looking for something. He rubbed her fingers together.

"Do you have a cigarette?" he asked.

"I'm sorry; this is a no smoking facility."

He rolled his eyes seemingly annoyed by my response.

"Please continue."

"As I said before he was my lover. We found each other after his wife died, was killed. I can't remember the details. He found his son with his wife or something like that. I being the woman that I am, thought I could tolerate one child, but then out of nowhere he tells me about a daughter."

"So what happened next?"

"I did what I could, but he seemed to prefer the little bitch over me. I became close with his son; he was lonely most of the time."

"What made you think he was lonely?"

"I could just tell; he hated the way his father loved on his precious little Ana as much as I did. So one day I told Robert to..."

"Don't say another word!"

Robert stood up from the chair causing it to flip, with his eyes locked straight ahead. The room felt cold. The cleaning crew must have been nearby as a strong smell of bleach began to seep into the room.

"Robert can you hear me."

"Have you ever thought about dying doc?" Robert asked.

"I think we all have at some point and time Robert. What makes you ask?"

"I have been trying for years to get away from all of them, but the harder I try the stronger they become. It's like they prefer her over me. "

"Prefer who Robert?"

He paused before Emalee took over.

"Doctor, you can clearly see that my patient has had enough, he is tired and needs to rest."

There was another brief silence, and I could feel the energy in the room change. Robert grabbed the sides of his head and let out a wail, but it wasn't just one voice, it was like a chorus. He screamed until he collapsed into a heap on the floor. He positioned himself on his knees as he sat back on his heels. For the first time since this all began there was a change in Robert. He had always been present despite *The Others* taking over. Despite his transformation into Ana there were always indicators of Robert's presence around. The person occupying the current space was clearly different.

"Are you afraid?" The unknown voice asked.

There were feminine mannerism but the voice was distinctly male.

"No I am not afraid." I responded, though my curiosity had been peaked.

"There is a common failure with people like us." He said as he began to rise to his feet.

"People like us?"

"People who treat people; people who gather evidence."

"I'm not following you."

"I didn't think you could." he responded snidely.

"Where are *The Others*?" I asked.

He began to walk around the chair as he spoke.

"*The Others* are gone."

"Gone where?"

"They have fused together you could say. They are locked away."

The previous smirk on Robert's face was now displayed prominently on the unidentified persona.

'Am I able to speak with, Robert, Ana, or Dr. White?"

"There is no need, they don't need you anymore. They have me and I will treat them."

"Emalee, I am glad to see that you were able to join us."

"Join you, I never left."

There was something about his tone that was dark. The entire time that Emalee was present over the years, she had been pleasant almost helpful when dealing with the others. Her voice always remained light and airy and she often postured effortlessly. The person now in the room claiming to be Emalee was male in stature, voice and demeanor, it was quiet puzzling.

"Well Emalee, as I was asking the group about Edward."

He tilted his head from side to side as the bones in his neck made a loud crackling sound which vibrated through our the room.

"The fire engine, do you have my fire engine." He demanded.

"Yes, it's in my office. I will give it to you after our session."

"No you will bring it to me now, and this is not a session. I am not your patient."

"Let's talk first and then I will return the truck."

"It's not a truck it's a fire engine."

"Emalee, do you know what happened to Johnathan and Dr. Allison?

He turned sharply before demanding the engine again.

"Bring me the engine and then we can talk."

Begrudgingly, the session was paused so that the engine could be retrieved. Only a few moments passed, and when I returned to the room Dr. Emalee Lieon and *The Others* were gone.

It was a beautiful day and Dr. Lieon felt refreshed and renewed. She was stronger than ever. Things were quiet and she hadn't heard from Ana, Robert or *The Others* in quite some time. With her new found freedom she was eager to get back to work. She walked across the courtyard to a gray building. She pushed through the double doors to find a redhead receptionist with a crooked smile sitting behind a desk.

"Hello, I am Dr. Emalee Lieon. I am here to see Dr. Morrison."

The receptionist smiled as she jotted down Emalee's name. Emalee looked around the lobby before taking a seat near a young mother with her child. The young mother took notice of Emalee as she thumbed through the mutilated magazines. Emalee was tall with one brown eye and one green eye. Her hair was dark brown and she was tall with an odd smile.

"Have you been here before?"

"No, I am here for an interview, I am a psychiatrist."

"That must be a fascinating line of work."

"It is; I am able to help a lot of people. So what brings you here?"

"It's my son Robert, he is a little different. He hasn't been the same since his father died."

The small boy with the sandy blonde hair was playing on the floor with a little red fire engine. He looked up at Emalee and quickly looked away as she smiled.

"I hope you don't mind, but that scarf you are wearing is lovely."

"Thank you."

"I would kill for a scarf like that."

"I would to, it was my mother's," the young lady said as she looked back at Emalee.

"By the way I am Ana." The young mother reached out her hand.

Emalee stared at the young mother with disdain as her name was paged over the intercom.

Dr. Lieon, paging

Dr. Lieon.....